For Victoria, Flinn, Freya, and Nat
G.A.

For Melanie, Gerry, Jack, and Luke
V.C.

Library of Congress Cataloging-in-Publication Data
is available from the Library of Congress.

Originally published in the United Kingdom by Orchard Books,
an imprint of the Watts Publishing Group, London.

Text © 2001 by Purple Enterprises.
Illustrations © 2001 by Vanessa Cabban.
Published in 2002 by Albert Whitman & Company, 6340 Oakton Street, Morton Grove, Illinois 60053-2723.
Published simultaneously in Canada by General Publishing, Limited, Toronto.
Printed in Singapore.
10 9 8 7 6 5 4 3 2 1

There's a HOUSE inside my MOMMy

Written by
Giles Andreae

Illustrated by
Vanessa Cabban

Albert Whitman & Company
Morton Grove, Illinois

There's a house inside my mommy
Where my little brother grows,
Or maybe it's my little sister,
No one really knows.

My daddy says I lived there too
When I was being made,
But I don't remember very much
About it, I'm afraid.

He always likes to tell me
It's a lovely place to be,
He knows because he's seen it
On the hospital's TV.

It's very warm and cozy
But because there's not a bed,
There's a sort of giant bathtub
Where the baby sleeps instead.

He needs to have a lot of room
To help him grow and play,
And that's why Mommy's tummy house
Gets bigger every day.

The house must have a kitchen
So he doesn't get too thin,
And I think the food my mommy eats
Can find its way to him.

He seems to want such funny things
But Mommy's very kind,
So she eats all sorts of crazy stuff
And doesn't seem to mind.

I try to help take care of her
And see she gets some rest,
Sometimes she even falls asleep
Before she gets undressed.

Sometimes Mommy feels so sick
I don't know what to do,
But if I had a house in *me*
I'd feel all yucky too.

I wish the house had windows
So that we could see inside,
I couldn't find a single one
No matter how I tried.

I'd like to show him all my toys
And let him see the view,
And point out the amazing things
I'll teach him how to do.

Sometimes me and Mommy
Like to cuddle on our own,
And I tell him that I love him
Through her tummy telephone.

I'm sure that he can hear me
And he likes the way I sound,
'Cause we see him kick his little feet
And somersault around.

I just can't wait to meet him!
I hope that he's all right.
My daddy says be patient
As the door is still shut tight.

Look who Mommy made for us—
My lovely little brother!
There's no one in her tummy now...
UNTIL SHE MAKES ANOTHER!